Disney · PIXAR

TOY STORY 3

Andy will soon be going away to college. He hasn't played with his toys in a long time. When he packs up his boxes, he will bring these things instead.

baseball glove

skateboard

stereo

cell phone

laptop

electric guitar

headphones

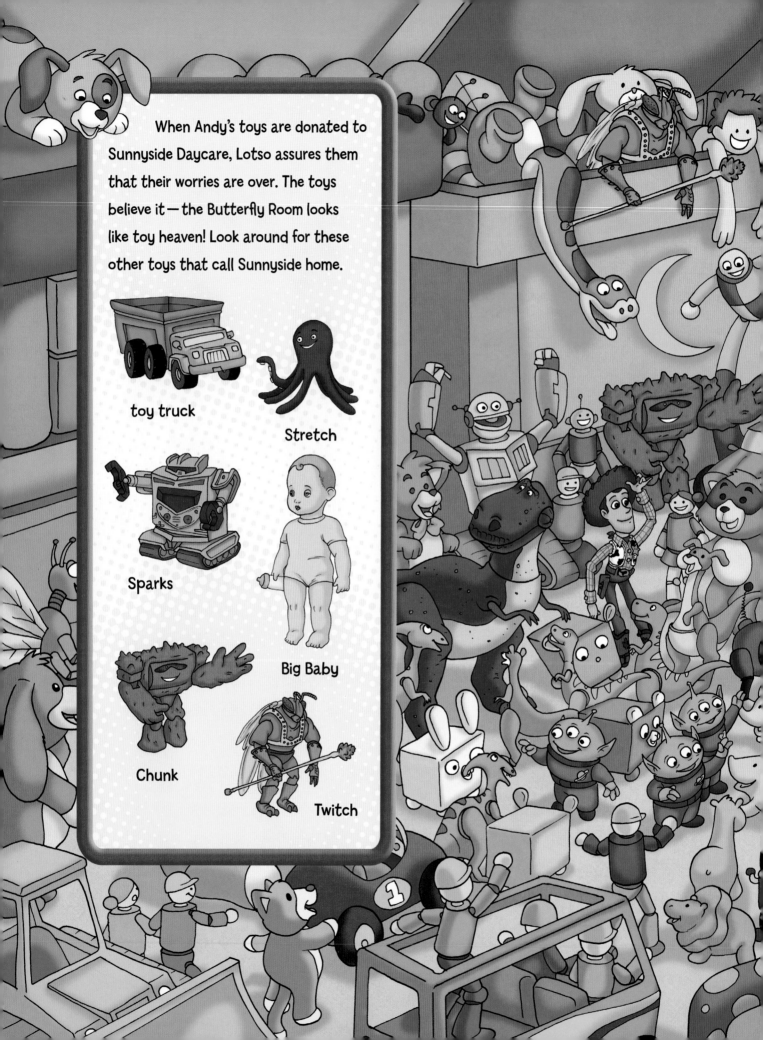

When Andy's toys are donated to Sunnyside Daycare, Lotso assures them that their worries are over. The toys believe it — the Butterfly Room looks like toy heaven! Look around for these other toys that call Sunnyside home.

toy truck

Stretch

Sparks

Big Baby

Chunk

Twitch

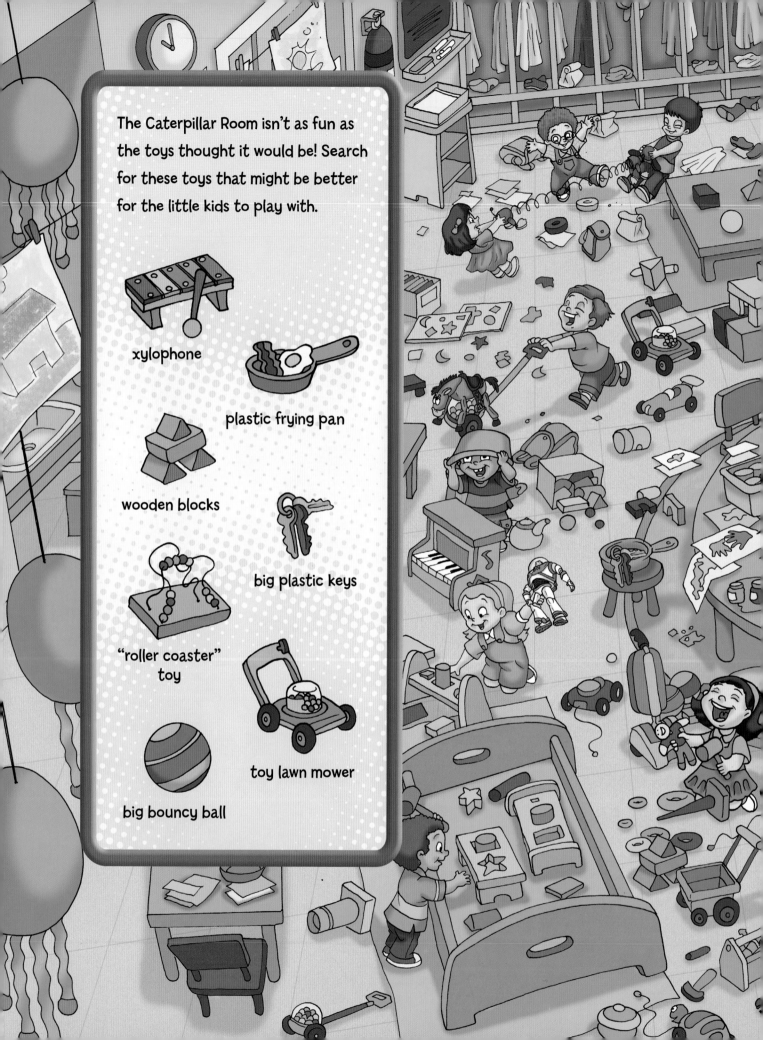

The Caterpillar Room isn't as fun as the toys thought it would be! Search for these toys that might be better for the little kids to play with.

xylophone

plastic frying pan

wooden blocks

big plastic keys

"roller coaster" toy

toy lawn mower

big bouncy ball

Bonnie finds Woody outside of Sunnyside and decides to take him home. She introduces Woody to her other toys and serves them all lunch. Find these colorful items from Bonnie's kitchen set.

purple teapot

blue teacup

pink plate

yellow bowl

red tumbler

green pitcher

Lotso's guards won't let the toys leave the Caterpillar Room. But the guards don't know that Woody has returned to rescue his friends! They don't belong in the storage bins. Find these art supplies that do.

bundle of pipe cleaners

jar of paint

safety scissors

glue

paintbrush

box of crayons

jar of glitter

Woody helped his friends escape from the Caterpillar Room. Now they just have to make it across the playground without being spotted by one of the guards. Search the playground to see where they've hidden!

this Alien

Rex

Jessie

Slinky Dog

Bullseye

Woody

Hamm

Buzz

The toys escape Sunnyside in a garbage truck, and the truck dumps them in a landfill. Ending up here is every toy's greatest fear! Hunt for these broken toys that Woody and his friends see.

headless doll

action figure

toy truck

stuffed panda

football

toy horse

When Woody realizes that Andy will never forget him, he decides that all the toys should stick together...at Bonnie's house! Look around the yard to find these toys that already live there.

Peas-in-a-Pod

Mr. Pricklepants

Buttercup

Trixie

Chuckles

Dolly

What will happen to Andy's toys after he leaves for college? Return to Andy's room to find these toys that are worried about the future.

Hamm

Bullseye

Slinky Dog

Jessie

Buzz

Rex

Rex loves meeting new friends! Go back to the Butterfly Room to find these small dinos that look up to him.

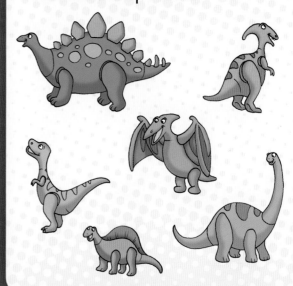

Wriggle back to the Caterpillar Room to look for these toddlers having a wild time!

Revisit Bonnie's bedroom to find these pictures that she drew.

Scoot back to the storage bins to find some things that the daycare children forgot and left behind.

juice box

baseball hat

sneaker

umbrella

sock

lunch bag

barrette

As the toys make their escape, they take care to move silently. Help them look out for these things that they won't want to step on or bump into.

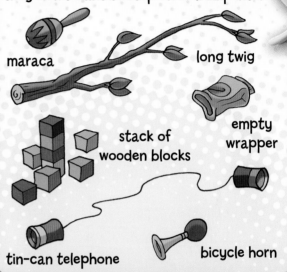

maraca

long twig

stack of wooden blocks

empty wrapper

tin-can telephone

bicycle horn

Slip back to the landfill to find these metal objects that will be collected and recycled.

hammer

pot

old lunch box

golf club

can

alarm clock

Andy's toys are sure to have lots of great adventures with Bonnie. Look around Bonnie's yard to find these things she might wear when she plays with them.

tutu

fairy wings

red cape

cowgirl hat

construction hat

monster mask

rainbow wig